The Owls of Blossom Wood

First published in the UK in 2016 by Scholastic Children's Books

An imprint of Scholastic Ltd
Euston House, 24 Eversholt Street
London, NW1 1DB, UK
Registered office: Westfield Road, Southam, Warwickshire, CV47 0RA
SCHOLASTIC and associated logos are trademarks and/or registered
trademarks of Scholastic Inc.

ISBN 978 1407 15668 2

A CIP catalogue record for this book is available from the British Library

Printed and bound by CPI Group (UK) Ltd, Croydon, CR0 4YY
Papers used by Scholastic Children's Books are made from wood
grown in sustainable forests.

5 7 9 10 8 6

www.scholastic.co.uk

The Owls of Blossom Wood

An Enchanted Wedding

Catherine Coe

SCHOLASTIC

For Isabelle Grace Henry,
with lots of love xxx

With many thanks to the amazing team at the

Fritton Owl Sanctuary for your invaluable support –

and to your wonderful, inspirational owls.

Chapter 1

Fancy Dress

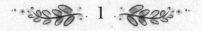

"Da da da-da, da, da da-da!" sung Katie, as Eva shuffled along the attic in an old wedding dress. The train was as long as the dress itself, and Alex grabbed it from behind before Eva tripped up on it.

"Whose dress was this?" Eva asked as she spun around at one end of the attic, pulling Alex with her. "These sleeves

are huge!" She looked at the lacy, puffy
material and giggled.

"I think it was my gran's." Katie
laughed. "She and Grandad got married
in the eighties. Mum's is in here
somewhere too!" Katie stuck her head
into the fancy-dress box and began pulling
out all sorts of dresses, skirts and hats.

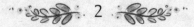

Meanwhile, Alex let go of the wedding dress train and went over to the little attic window. She sighed deeply and rolled her big brown eyes. "Alfie's still out there!"

Eva scooted over to stand beside Alex and pulled back the veil on her head over her brown bobbed hair. "Why does he have to play right next to the tree trunk?"

"Because that's what brothers do," came a mumbling from the fancy-dress box. "Anything that's SUPER annoying!"

The three best friends desperately wanted to look inside the hollow tree trunk that lay at the bottom of Katie's garden. They were waiting for a special feather to be left out for them. A feather that would magically whisk them away

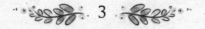

to the incredible Blossom Wood. But
Alfie had set up a hideout beside the
tree trunk, and they didn't want to check
inside it with him around – because he
might wonder what they were doing and
find out about their secret adventures.

"The feather could have been there all
morning," said Eva, her green eyes wide.
"And we don't know!"

"Aha!" Katie's head emerged from the
box, and she spun around to her friends,
her blue eyes glistening. "But maybe I
could distract him with this!" She held
up a cowboy hat in the air.

"Good plan, Katie," said Alex in her
soft voice. "He's *so* going to want to
wear that hat!" Katie passed it to Alex
and she plopped it on top of her black
curly hair, which was done up in a bun.
As Alex turned back to the window,

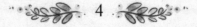

it wobbled about on the bun like a spinning plate.

Katie jumped up and joined Alex, pushing down the dusty sash window and cupping her hands to her mouth. "Alfie, look what we've found!"

Alfie's blond head popped out between the folds of a red sun lounger he'd made into a tent. "A cowboy hat! Brilliant! Can you bring it down?"

Katie shook her head and grinned. "Um ... no, sorry. You'll have to come and get it!"

"You're so annoying!" Alfie replied, slithering from his hideout like a snake into the long grass.

Katie turned to Eva and Alex. "Come on – quick!"

Alex tossed the hat to the floor like a frisbee, and they jumped down the

rickety attic stairs as quickly as they could, with Eva still in the wedding gown. Alex grabbed the train again – Eva was without a doubt the clumsiest of the three friends, and Alex didn't want her to trip on it!

As they reached the landing and swerved around the bannister towards the stairs, Alfie appeared at the bottom. He climbed up the wooden steps like a monkey, shouting, "Where are you going?" as the girls passed him the other way.

"None of your business!" Katie said as she ran down the hallway. They darted through the kitchen towards the back door, Alex still holding the wedding train tightly.

"Ooh, who's the lucky groom?" Katie's dad joked as he pulled a can of tuna out of a kitchen cupboard. "Don't be

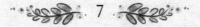

too long – lunch will be ready soon. Or should I say the wedding breakfast?"

Katie sighed. Her dad was always making silly jokes.

"We won't be long," Alex told Katie's dad politely, knowing that even if the feather was there, and they were whisked off to Blossom Wood, no time would pass at home. They wouldn't need to worry about being late for lunch.

Alex jumped out of the door last and ran down the garden behind Eva, past the rose bed, rabbit hutch and greenhouse. Katie was already diving into the hollow tree trunk, but Eva and Alex were much slower – the wedding dress slowed them down as they ran, although it was quicker than taking it off. It had taken them ages to lace up the back of it!

"Quick," echoed the voice of Katie

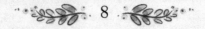

from inside the trunk. "It's here!"

As she shuffled across the lawn, Eva
tingled all over. They were going to
Blossom Wood again! She climbed into

the trunk more carefully than normal, not wanting to damage the wedding dress. In the darkness, Katie's cheeks were ruby red with excitement, framed by her long blonde hair. Katie held a glossy white feather in one hand, and took Eva's hand with the other.

"Where are you going?" came Alfie's voice as Alex jumped into the tree trunk last and grabbed Eva's outstretched hand. Katie's younger brother was chasing after them – they'd only just made it.

Holding hands, the three best friends shut their eyes tight, and waited for the familiar spinning and swirling to begin…

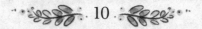

Chapter 2

A Special Request

"We're here!" Eva breathed as she opened her eyes and waved her wings in the air. For she was no longer a girl but a barn owl! Every time the three best friends went to Blossom Wood, after spinning and swirling and whooshing and whirling in the hollow tree, they magically turned from girls into *owls*.

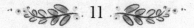

To her left, Alex balanced on the same
tree branch as Eva, her beak stretched
into a smile. Alex was a little owl, brown
and fluffy, and half the size of Eva. To
Eva's right, Katie hopped from talon to
talon, making the branch bounce. She
was the biggest of the three – an elegant

snowy owl, with huge white wings.

Katie had already spotted one of their woodlander friends, a badger called Bobby. He was the one who usually left the feather out for them. She tipped her head down and glided off the branch, beaming as she floated in the air on her giant wings. To Katie, flying was even more fun than ballet dancing!

As she reached the ground, landing gently on a carpet of crunchy autumnal leaves, she noticed Bobby was smiling just as much as her. *Phew*, she thought with relief. The girls were usually called to Blossom Wood when the animals needed their help. But it didn't look as if anything was seriously wrong.

"Blossom Wood looks gorgeous in the autumn," hooted Alex as she landed beside Katie on the forest floor. The tree

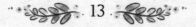

that they'd arrived on, called the Moon
Chestnut because of its curved trunk, was
covered in shiny golden-yellow leaves.
Around them, the trees in the wood had
transformed into their autumn colours –
red, orange and gold. Alex had thought
the wood looked beautiful in the spring,
when the trees were covered in blossoming
flowers, but this was just as stunning.

"Is everything OK?" Eva asked as she landed a bit too close to Bobby and he put out a paw to steady her.

"I think so," said Bobby in his gravelly voice. "But we do need you for something…"

"What is it?" Katie began to frown, wondering if there was something the matter after all. Maybe Bobby was putting on a fake smile so he didn't worry them.

"We were wondering if you'd mind awfully … if it's not too much of a problem … if you'd take part in the very special wedding ceremony that's happening today?"

Eva did a little hop of excitement. "Someone's getting married? Who is it?"

Bobby grinned. "It's the otters of Willow Lake – do you know them? Actually, you probably haven't met

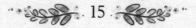

them before because they're rather shy, and tend to stay in the water. But it's traditional for owls to deliver the wedding rings to any marriage, and now you wonderful owls are a part of Blossom Wood, I just *had* to ask!"

"We'd love to!" said Alex, while at the same time thinking, *How on earth do otters wear wedding rings?*

"Otters have wedding rings?" blurted out Katie, who didn't always think before she spoke.

Luckily, Bobby didn't seem to think the question was impolite, and just smiled. "Of a kind, yes, but not on their paws – no doubt they'd slip off in the water! They wear special wedding rings around their necks, made from dandelion seeds."

"Oh, they sound so pretty!" twittered

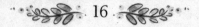

Eva, wondering how they were made. Perhaps she could try making them at home – she loved crafts and often created bits of jewellery for her friends.

Alex tilted her head to one side. "What's that noise?" she asked, her big yellow eyes still as she concentrated.

The animals were quiet for a moment.

"I can't hear anything," said Bobby, shaking his stripy head. "Though sadly my hearing is not what it once was. A sign of getting old, unfortunately!"

"I can hear it too," said Eva. It was a low, hooting sort of sound – a bit like a kazoo. They hadn't heard anything else quite like it in Blossom Wood before.

Katie looked up … up … up … to where it was coming from. "Is that an OWL?"

As the three best friends were the only

owls that came to the forest, this was very strange indeed. But Katie was right, thought Alex – she could see the brown-and-white speckled feathers of an owl nestled in the crook of a branch.

"H-hello?" said Bobby. "Are you OK?" He seemed just as surprised as they were.

At that moment, the owl fluttered its flecked wings and launched itself out of the tree. But it didn't so much fly as fall, and Alex put a wing over her eyes as the owl landed in a ball at their feet, scattering the autumn leaves everywhere.

"Where am I?" the owl said as it uncurled itself and stood up unsteadily.

Katie clapped a wing to her mouth. She'd recognize that voice anywhere. "Alfie!"

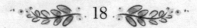

Alfie's yellow eyes grew huge. "Katie?"
he squeaked. He rushed to his sister
and she wrapped her snowy wings tight
around him.

"What are you doing here?" Katie asked.

"I ... erm ... I ... followed you into
the tree trunk, and ... and then there
was all this spinning and whirling and
wind ... and suddenly I was here!"
Alfie's face poked out from under Katie's

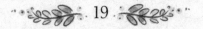

wing and he swivelled his head around.
"Where are we?"

"This is Blossom Wood!" twittered
Eva. "Isn't it beautiful?"

"But what's Blossom Wood?" He
looked down at himself. "And why are
we all owls?"

Alex wasn't really sure about the answer to his second question. Alfie was certainly an owl – a long-eared owl, in fact. She recognized those cute pointy ear tufts from one of her wildlife books. But she had no idea why they magically turned to owls when they were here.

"Can we go home now?" Alfie added, his yellow eyes darting about uncertainly.

"We'll go back soon," Katie whispered, so that Bobby didn't hear. The badger didn't know that Alex, Eva and Katie came from somewhere else entirely, where they weren't owls but girls. They'd tried to explain it once but he hadn't understood. Katie put her wingtips on each of Alfie's shoulders and looked into his eyes. "We have to deliver the rings for a wedding first. But I think you'll have fun here – it's

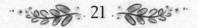

an amazing place. And now you're an owl, you can fly!"

Alfie looked around again. "But it's huge," he said in a wobbly voice. "I want to go back to our garden!"

Katie sighed. Alfie was always pestering to play with them, but now he was here, he wanted to go home! She understood it might seem a bit scary at first – how could she explain that being in Blossom Wood was always wonderful?

"Oh, hello!" A sudden high-pitched voice made them all turn around. It was Loulou the squirrel, scampering along the woodland path towards them. She skidded to a stop and grinned at Alfie. "Oh! I haven't seen you before! I'm Loulou!" She curtsied, just like she'd done the first time Katie, Eva and Alex had arrived in Blossom Wood. Then she

held out a paw to shake Alfie's wing.

He looked at the grinning Loulou, then down at her paw, and smiled. He stuck out a wing slowly and they shook hands. "I-I'm Alfie," he said, sounding shocked to meet a talking squirrel, but not quite as frightened as before.

With her other paw, Loulou brought out an acorn-shaped lollipop from behind her back. "Would you like this?"

Now Alfie beamed. "Yes, please!" Loulou passed it to him while winking to the others, and soon Alfie was nibbling at it with his little beak.

Bobby lumbered closer to Alfie then, kicking up the crunchy leaves on the ground. "We are so very pleased to have you in Blossom Wood, Alfie," he said seriously. "I do hope you'll stay for a while?"

Alfie nodded mid-bite. "Thank you, Mr Badger," he said.

Bobby chuckled. "Oh, my, that makes me sound even older than I am! You must call me Bobby." He turned to the owls. "Now, let me introduce you to the otters. They'll be thrilled that you're here!"

Chapter 3
Meet the Otters

"Are you ready to fly, Alfie?" Alex asked him gently.

Alfie's long ears turned down in a worried sort of way. "I-I don't know. I wasn't very good at it just then! Is it difficult?"

Before anyone could reply, a ball of fluff shot out from under a

nearby blackberry hedge. "Owls! You're back!"

Eva giggled as the ball uncurled into a little grey rabbit in front of them. "Billy! How are you?"

"Very well, thank you," Billy said politely as his cheeks went pink. The young rabbit always seemed in awe of the owls. "Except ... I was hoping to play appleball, but none of my brothers and sisters want to." He hung his head, looking sad. "Will you play with me?"

Katie put a wing on Billy's shoulder. "Oh, I'd really love to." And she meant it – it sounded like a lot of fun. "But we need to go and see the otters."

"I'll play!" Alfie hooted, his eyes brighter now. Katie smiled, relieved that her brother was getting back to his usual self.

Billy twitched his whiskers happily. "Really? Great!" The bunny grabbed Alfie's wingtip with his paw and they began running over to a nearby clearing.

Katie winked at the others. "I think Alfie's going to be OK!" she said.

Bobby rubbed his black paws together. "OK, then – let's pay that visit to the

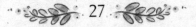

otters! If you fly to Willow Lake, I'll meet you there as soon as I can."

Eva, Alex and Katie nodded and waved goodbye to Loulou, who was soon darting up the chestnut tree to her nest. They hopped, skipped and jumped, fluttering their wings to take off into the air. Bobby was soon just a stripy dot on the ground below them.

"See you soon!" Eva called down to the badger, not looking where she was going and almost flying into a small branch of the Moon Chestnut tree. Luckily, Katie pulled it out of the way just in time. "Thanks!" Eva said with a grin.

The three best friends zoomed over the treetops, taking in the most incredible view of Blossom Wood as they flew. The autumnal trees looked even prettier from up here – like a red and gold rug

spread across the entire wood. On the forest floor, they spotted lots of creatures dashing about.

"Do you think they're preparing for the wedding?" tweeted Alex. With her fantastic owl eyesight she could see some of the deer down near Foxglove Glade arranging flowers.

Katie nodded. "I think so!"

With the water of Willow Lake glittering just in front of them, the friends began their descent, tilting their heads forward and slowing down their wings. For fun, Katie flipped a loop the loop and then did a cartwheel in the air.

Alex smiled. "You'll have to show Alfie how you can do that. He'll be so impressed!"

They landed beside one of the many

willow trees that surrounded the large lake, to a chorus of quacking amongst the lakeside reeds.

A brown female duck came waddling through the weeds and smiled.

Eva recognized this duck from the last time they were in Blossom Wood. She had a long name that Eva would never be able to remember, but luckily she'd been happy for them to use a shortened version!

"Hello, Hampty!" said Katie. "Are you helping get ready for the wedding too?"

The duck nodded. "Oh, yes, quack! We're making reed ribbons to decorate the lake." She fluttered her purplish wings. "It's so exciting – quack quack! We haven't had a wedding in the wood for absolutely ages!"

Alex bobbed her head in agreement. It

was very exciting to be at a wedding –
especially one in Blossom Wood! She
wondered what the wedding would be
like – and *where* it would be, since otters
spent all their time in the water...

"We've come to say hello to the
otters," Eva told Hampty. "Do you know
where we can find them?"

Hampty's husband, Monty, poked his
glossy green head out from the reeds
then, and pointed a white wing across
the lake. "They'll be over there, on the
other side. They don't stray very far from
home, you see – they're too shy for that."

"Thanks, Monty," twittered Alex. "See
you later at the wedding!"

Eva, Katie and Alex took off again,
flying straight over Willow Lake, which
glistened in the autumn sunshine. As
they neared the opposite edge, Katie

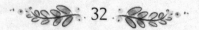

spotted a familiar figure plodding along.
"Hey, Bobby," she hooted, and he looked
up, smiled and waved.

They landed beside him, close to the
water, and Bobby led them towards a little
sandy cove at the lakeside. Alex sucked in
a breath of excitement as she spotted two
small heads – a little way out, the otter
couple were swimming about in the water.

"Sammy? Jo?" Bobby called gently. "I've

brought some creatures to meet you…"

The otters dipped their heads and began heading for the shore. Eva's feathers prickled like goosebumps as she waited to meet the otters. She'd never seen one before. Katie hopped from foot to foot, and Alex bobbed her head so fast she knew she must look like the nodding dog on her mum's desk. They were all *so* excited, and she thought the otters would be too.

But when the otters' heads reappeared above the water, their eyes looked so, so sad.

"Whatever's wrong?" asked Bobby. "Aren't you pleased to see the owls?"

Both otters squeaked out a long whine and one of them wiped its eyes with its paw.

The other one spoke first. "It's not that − not at all − we're so happy the owls are here to take part in our

wedding and deliver the rings!"

"But that's the problem," said the other otter, with a voice so sad Alex thought her heart might break into thousands of pieces. "Our wedding rings have gone missing. We're not going to be able to get married after all!"

Chapter 4

A Very Big Problem

The owls turned to Bobby. His mouth gaped open – he was speechless.

Katie fluttered closer to the otters, wanting to comfort them in some way. "But where have they gone?"

"We don't know, do we, Jo?" said one of the otters, who must have been Sammy. "We left them hanging on a

willow tree while we had a little swim and practised our vows."

"When we got back, they'd vanished – just like that!" added Jo.

"Oh dear. Oh dear, oh dear, oh dear," said Bobby finally. He rubbed at his forehead with a paw, shook his head slowly, then took a deep breath. "But don't worry, otters. The owls are here. And they can help with anything." He turned to Eva, Alex and Katie. "You'll be able to fix this, won't you?"

The three best friends looked at each other. They had no idea where the missing wedding rings might be. *But we have to try to help*, thought Eva.

Alex swivelled her fluffy head to search the ground around them. There was no sign of the rings whatsoever. "Can you tell us what they look like?" she asked.

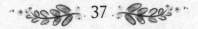 37

Sammy nodded shyly. "They're made
of sparkling dandelion seeds – from the
dandelion puffs that grow around Badger
Falls."

"The beavers are the ones who make
them into rings – they weave the

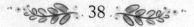

seeds together with their teeth," Bobby explained. "It's very clever."

"We only left them for a few minutes," said Jo quietly. "I don't know who would take them!"

Katie could see tears springing in Jo's eyes. "Your wedding WILL go ahead," she told the otters. "We'll get you your wedding rings, no matter what it takes!"

"Oh, thank you, owls," said Sammy, grabbing Jo's hand. "We've been so excited about our wedding for so long. Everyone has come here today especially, including many creatures from way beyond the Great Hedge!" The otters lay backwards in the water, side by side, and floated away.

Eva could hear them practising their wedding vows in the distance. *Oh, we*

have to make sure they get to say them for real! she thought.

"Can we use something else for the rings?" Alex asked Bobby when the otters were out of earshot.

He shook his head. "I'm afraid not. A wedding wouldn't be official without the

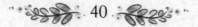

dandelion-seed rings. You see, in Blossom Wood we believe dandelions are magical, representing the passing of time in a day. The rings are a symbol of being together for ever."

"Do you mean because you can use them to tell the time?" twittered Eva. She, Alex and Katie loved doing that at home – blowing the seeds from dandelion puffs and counting how long it took to blow them all away. Although they didn't get it right very much.

"No, no – although the young woodlanders here do enjoy doing that. Indeed, I did too, when I was a nipper, many years ago. No, they're special because as the dandelion grows and changes, it first looks like the sun when it's a flower, then the moon when it's

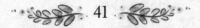

41

a puff, then it turns to stars when the dandelion seeds are blown away."

Alex bobbed her fluffy head. "Oh wow, that does make dandelions sound *very* special." She'd never thought of them in that way before, but she would from now on!

Katie flapped her wings and set her beak in a determined line. "So where should we look first?"

Alex looked about the lake, wondering where to start, and gasped. "What's that?"

Eva, Katie and Bobby turned to follow her gaze – to the branches of a silver willow tree. Alex was already fluttering up towards it. "I can't see anything!" Bobby said from the ground.

But with her brilliant owl eyesight, Alex had spotted what looked like dandelion seeds scattered across the drooping willow branches. As she

got closer, she scooped them all up on her wing, then soared back down to the others.

Bobby bent his head towards Alex's wing to inspect them. "They're the dandelion seeds all right. Look how they sparkle."

"But who would have broken the wedding rings?" twittered Katie, putting her wings on her hips. "It's such a nasty thing to do."

"Oh, oh, oh, I think I might know the answer to that," came a tweet from behind them. A yellow-winged goldfinch appeared between the willow leaves. "My little chicks were hungry, and as they're only hopping yet – not flying – I went to get some food for them. But it seems they couldn't wait – when I got back, our nest was scattered with dandelion seeds."

Eva's beak fell open. "But didn't they know they were the wedding rings?"

The goldfinch shook her head. "I don't think so – they're not very old, you see. I'd hoped they were just normal dandelion seeds, not the ones from the wedding rings, but then I overheard you talking to the otters and ... well ... I'm so sorry!"

Alex hopped over to the goldfinch and gave her a hug. "It's not your fault. And

your chicks weren't to know either. It's just a terrible mistake." She looked up, trying to see the goldfinch's nest. "Are there many seeds left? Perhaps we can use them to make new rings without too much trouble."

Bobby's black eyes brightened. "That sounds like an excellent idea."

But when the owls flew up with the goldfinch to investigative the nest, there were only about ten dandelion seeds there – and five guilty-looking chicks with round yellow bellies.

"I don't think that's going to be enough," said Katie. "Especially not for two rings."

"Kids, what were you doing?" The mother goldfinch shook her head at her little chicks in the nest.

"We're sorry!" they twittered.

"We didn't know they were special."

"We were just so hungry!"

The mother sighed. "You're *always* hungry. You'd eat the nest itself if I didn't keep an eye on you!" She turned to the owls. "Let me help you find new wedding rings for the otters – I feel terrible!"

Eva shook her heart-shaped head. "No, no – you must stay here and look after your chicks. As you say, you don't want

them eating the nest! And please don't feel bad — it was a mistake."

Alex put a wing out to Eva and Katie. "We should get going — we don't have long before the wedding." She cupped the remaining dandelion seeds in her talons carefully, and fluttered back down to the ground.

Bobby's face fell as the owls landed and he saw how few dandelion seeds Alex carried. But Katie wasn't about to give up. She put her wings on her hips. "We'll just have to move to plan B — find some more dandelion seeds!"

"You said they grow at Badger Falls, right?" Alex asked Bobby.

"Yes, that's right. But…"

"So we have to go there right away!" hooted Eva. Before Bobby could finish what he was saying, the desperate owls

were already flying up into the bright
blue sky, their sights fixed on the
sparkling water of Badger Falls in
the distance.

Chapter 5
Tick, Tock, Dandelion Clock

Badger Falls was a beautiful place. The water crashed down from Echo Mountains and Eva thought it looked like the prettiest, most enormous shower, in between bright green plants clinging on to the mountainside. The falling water sparkled like sequins in the sun, and as it splashed down, it fed into Rushing

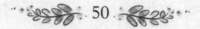

River — which wove across Blossom Wood all the way to Willow Lake.

Eva landed beside the waterfall and began looking for dandelion puffs straight away. But there were only plants and grass here — she couldn't see any dandelion seeds. *Maybe I'm not searching hard enough*, she thought, fluttering over to the other side of the waterfall and getting sprinkled by the falling water as she flew. But there were none here either.

"Where are they all?" said Katie, zooming higher up the waterfall to see if she could find any there.

"I don't know — usually they're so easy to find!" twittered Alex. That was the case in her garden at home, anyway — her dad was always complaining about dandelions messing up his lawn! Alex

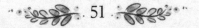

liked the pretty yellow flowers, and
how they transformed into dandelion
puffs like magic, even if her dad called
them *weeds*!

Katie flew up and down, her orange
eyes fixed on the ground,
hoping that one
would pop
up from
somewhere.
"Well, there
are none
here. But
Bobby

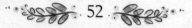

definitely said this is where they grew."

Eva put a wing to her forehead. "Oh! Wait, Bobby was trying to say something as we left…"

It was as if a light had pinged on in Alex's head as she realized something. "He must have been trying to tell us that there were no more left!" She stared at the grass harder, and noticed there were what looked like dandelion *stalks* poking up between the fronds of grass – but no seeds.

"Oh no…" Katie slumped back on to the grass, feeling disappointment swallow her up like quicksand.

"But with no dandelion puffs, there are no dandelion seeds, and we need them to make the wedding rings!" Eva sat down too, still looking around her, although she'd lost all hope by now.

As her friends pulled glum faces, Alex

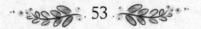

was busy thinking of what she knew about dandelions. They sprang up all over her garden at home, because the wind blew the seeds about, which then grew into new dandelions in the soil. Could some of the seeds have been blown somewhere else?

At that moment, a breeze rustled her feathers, as if it was a sign. Alex jumped up. "We have to search over there," she hooted, pointing in the direction the wind was blowing, towards the Oval of Oaks.

Katie had pushed herself up from the ground too. "What are you thinking, Alex?"

"Well, the wind blows dandelion seeds about easily, because they're so light. So if they've been blown across Blossom Wood, there might be some more dandelions sprouting in the place they landed!"

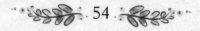

Eva jumped up and clapped her brown wings together. "Oh, you are so clever, Alex!"

Alex felt her cheeks redden. "Not really — I just like nature stuff, that's all!"

"So we follow the direction of the wind?" asked Katie, her hopes rising inside her like a hot-air balloon.

"Exactly!" Alex bobbed her tiny head, and the three friends began hopping away from Badger Falls, all the while looking for any signs of new dandelions.

They crossed a large patch of soil dotted with holes — this was where Bobby and the other badgers lived. There were no dandelions puffs there — just plain brown earth with the odd rock or log scattered about.

They kept on, still with the wind behind them. Alex knew that the

direction of the wind could often change,
but with nothing else to guide them,
she just had to hope that her hunch was
right. They neared the oak trees, which
were a mass of gorgeous fiery orange

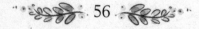

and red colours. Fallen leaves covered
the ground, making it harder to spot any
dandelion puffs, so the friends walked
extra slowly, looking very carefully.

"One, two, three…" came a hooting
voice.

"Four, five, six…" a different,
squeakier voice added.

"Who's that?" asked Alex quietly.

"Alfie!" Katie yelled as they rounded a
thick tree trunk and a long-eared owl and a
bunny rabbit came into view in the distance.

"It looks like Alfie and Billy are best
friends already!" said Eva. The pair were
jumping about in the rustling leaves,
laughing and giggling.

"Let's go and check on them," Alex
suggested, and fluttered up into the air
to reach them quickly. Her two friends
followed her lead.

As they landed, Katie gave out a squeal. "You found them! Dandelion puffs! Hundreds of them!"

Billy and Alfie played amongst a thick patch of sparkling dandelion puffs, each holding a bunch in their hands.

"So that's what you were counting," twittered Eva. "You were trying to tell the time by the number of blows!"

"And you found exactly what we're looking for – you boys are the best!" Alex felt mightily relieved that her instinct about the wind was right, and that it had blown the seeds here to grow into new dandelions. She began plucking up the dandelion puffs that grew at the edge of one of the oak trees.

Alfie and Billy looked at each other, clearly confused.

"Really?" said Alfie, who was much

more used to his sister and her friends complaining about him.

Katie put a white wing around her younger brother and explained why they needed the dandelion seeds. "Will you help us to collect them?" she finished.

The boys nodded furiously. "Of course!" squeaked Billy.

And so the owls and the rabbit began pulling up all the dandelion puffs that they could see, taking care not to blow away any of the seeds, even though it was *so* tempting.

After a few minutes, Katie said, "I think that's enough! We should get these over to the beavers now – so they can start making the wedding rings."

Alex looked up at the blue sky, where the sun was beginning to dip down towards the horizon. "Oh, I hope we have enough time. The otters *have* to get married today – so many creatures have come here especially for the wedding!"

Alex, Eva and Katie left Billy and Alfie to play, and flew off to find the beavers at Willow Lake.

"Wonderful!" cried Bobby, when the three best friends landed where they'd left him on the shore, clutching the dandelion puffs. The badger was now surrounded by hundreds of animals and birds and insects, all waiting patiently for the wedding. Katie didn't recognize a lot of them, but of course that was because many had come from outside Blossom Wood, like Sammy had said.

Eva spotted the otters, still swimming in the water. They moved slowly, holding hands.

"The beavers live just over there," the badger told them, pointing a paw towards one of the most incredible homes Alex had ever seen in Blossom Wood.

In the banks of the lake, the beavers had created a waterside lodge made from branches, logs and mud, built like a real house. It even looked as if it had two storeys!

"Thanks, Bobby!" Katie hooted, and the three friends flew over to the beavers. They recognized one of them, Jonny, right away.

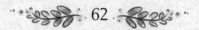

"We heard about the wedding rings,"
he squealed in his high-pitched voice.
"Did you manage to find more
dandelion seeds?"

They nodded, and held up the
dandelion puffs they'd gathered.

"But do we have enough time to make
two before the wedding?" asked Alex,

bobbing her head, which was full of worries.

Jonny twitched his nose and jumped from foot to foot. "I'm not sure." He looked down at the seeds. "They usually each take a least a day to make... But we beavers could make one while you owls make the other — and we can show you how to make it as we go along."

"But we only have a few hours!" Eva hooted, feeling desperation stir up inside her like a whirlpool.

"We have to make them in time, we just have to," twittered Alex.

Katie raised the dandelion puffs in her talons. "There's only one way to find out — let's get started!"

Chapter 6
The Wedding

The otters couldn't delay getting married any longer – not with all their guests waiting. Some of them had come a very long way – and they still had to get home again! The pinky-red sun had already sunk below the horizon, turning the sky an inky black, lit by a bright half-moon and twinkling stars.

They swam closer to the shore, still holding hands, towards the animals, birds and insects who were waiting for the wedding to begin. The creatures spoke in hushed, excited tones, since it wasn't every day that a wedding took place in Blossom Wood. No one – except the beavers, goldfinches and Bobby – knew that there was anything wrong. They had no idea that there might be no wedding rings, which would mean no wedding!

Bobby stood on the edge of the shore in his bow tie, waiting to conduct the ceremony. His stripy face was clouded by a frown, as he wondered if the owls and the beavers had managed to make the wedding rings in time. They were so delicate and fiddly that the beavers usually spent days working on them.

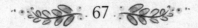

The wedding band started up on the banks of the lake and the woodlanders fell silent all of a sudden. Charles, a blackbird and the Blossom Wood music teacher, stood at the front, conducting the musicians, using a little twig which he swiped and swirled at the air. They were playing a bouncy jazz song, but they'd soon switch to the wedding march, which was the signal for the wedding rings to be delivered.

White wedding fireflies fluttered around the crowd and the lake water, lighting up the area like fairy magic. The guests oohed and ahhed at the sight, and many of the younger creatures jumped up and down with excitement.

"Do you think they'll be here in time?" asked Sammy from the water's edge.

Bobby looked down at the anxious otters. "Oh, I'm sure – we can always rely on the owls to save the day!"

Just as the badger turned back round, the crowd began to murmur. Everyone's heads were tilted up, looking at something above them. That was when Bobby jumped up in the air and kicked his heels together. For there were the owls, flying above the lake, with sparkling wedding rings in their beaks!

Katie, Eva and Alex soared over the wedding guests, despite feeling exhausted. They'd worked harder than they'd thought was possible to weave the dandelion seeds together, copying the beavers' every movement. Their beaks had bobbed up and down and left and right and back and forth – but they'd worked as a team, and that had made all the difference.

Bobby was beaming from white-tipped

ear to white-tipped ear, and Alex was sure she saw him do a heel-kick – even though the badger always said he was too old for dancing and such things! The wedding march began to play, and Alex smiled as she remembered Katie singing it earlier that day, in the attic. Now they really were at a wedding. A very special one in Blossom Wood!

As the owls landed, Eva spotted tears in the otters' brown eyes – but this time the tears were of joy. "Thank you, thank you!" they said, splashing the water with their paws and hugging tightly.

"Thank treetops for you, dear owls," said Bobby, taking the woven wedding rings from them with a bow. "I knew if anyone could do it, it'd be you!"

Katie managed a smile back, even though her beak ached from all the work

she'd been doing. "It's our pleasure," she said.

"Ours too!" hooted Eva and Alex together.

As the three friends found a space to sit amongst the crowd, Bobby looked out towards the wedding guests. "I need two helpers for the ceremony. Does anyone volunteer?"

At the front, two animals began jumping up and down, their hands in the air. Alex chuckled when she realized who it was. Alfie and Billy – of course!

Bobby waved them forward and passed them the wedding rings. "Please can you look after these until I ask for them?"

Katie winced. Her little brother wasn't the best at taking care of things. She

hoped after all their work he wouldn't
drop the ring or break it!

The band came to the end of the
wedding march song and Bobby raised
his arms up and coughed loudly. "Ahem!
Welcome, welcome, welcome. Today
is an extremely special day in Blossom
Wood, and I am delighted that you could
all make it – I know some of you have

come from very far away. I am thrilled to announce the wedding of Jo and Sammy Otter!"

The crowd clapped and whooped and cheered, the bees buzzed and the birds tweeted. All the fireflies swarmed towards the otters and fluttered above the water, lighting them up like a spotlight.

Bobby had to cough again to get the audience to calm down. When they finally quietened, he turned to the otters, who were still holding hands. "Jo and Sammy, you are here to be married, and to commit to loving and caring for each other for the rest of your lives."

The otters both nodded solemnly. "We are," they said together. "We promise to love and care for each other, in spring, summer, autumn and winter, until the end of our days."

"Then it's time for the rings."
Bobby tilted his head at Alfie and Billy.
They looked confused for a moment,
then realized what Bobby had said
and scampered over to the very edge
of the water.

"Alfie, please place the wedding ring
over Jo's head," Bobby instructed.

Alfie held up the ring slowly, and
hooked it gently over Jo.

Thank treetops for that! thought Katie.

Bobby looked at the young bunny.
"Billy, now your turn."

Billy squeaked as he placed the ring
over Sammy's brown head.

"Thank you, Alfie and Billy," Bobby
croaked. He turned back to the otters.
"Now, on the count of three, please bow
your heads together. This will signal your
bond – one that will stand the test of time."

Bobby swung around to the crowd. "After me…"

"One … two … three!" everyone hooted, squeaked, buzzed, bleated and tweeted.

The otters grinned at each other and tilted their heads together gently. Eva blinked in astonishment as the dandelion seeds of the rings suddenly lit up like fairy lights. *They must really be magical!* she thought, as the wedding rings continued to glow and sparkle like never before.

"You are now married!" announced Bobby, clapping his hands together and beaming. Everybody else joined in – with their paws, hooves, wings, legs and antennae.

The otters squeezed together in a hug, then swam backwards into the lake, still holding hands, their wedding rings

gleaming like magic. The crowd
became silent.

"What's happening now?" Eva
mouthed to Alex.

Before Alex could reply, Bobby

answered the question. "Please join me in watching the otters' first dance – the wedding party is about to begin!"

As Katie watched the dancing otters, she couldn't stop smiling – even though it made her face ache more. Jo and Sammy swam together like the best synchronized swimmers, twirling about, ducking down under the water, and doing somersaults, kicks and dives in the lake. *I want to learn to dance in the water like that*, Katie thought. *It looks like so much fun!*

The otters' dance came to an end and the band began a new tune, with the frog pine-cone drummers introducing the beat. Alex couldn't quite believe her eyes as the pretty green lily pads that were dotted about the lake started to magically draw together, like lots of magnets

attracting each other. Soon they'd knitted into one big lily-pad blanket across the water. The lily pads shone brightly beneath the white lights of the wedding fireflies.

"Wow," said Eva breathlessly, staring at the floating carpet.

"Don't be shy," Bobby told them. "It's our own Blossom Wood water dance floor. Try it out!"

And they did – together with all the other woodlanders who couldn't swim. Surprisingly, even with hundreds of creatures on the dance floor, it stayed afloat perfectly – a soft, springy mat that was perfect for dancing.

They danced and twirled and spun until the moon was high in the sky, when Katie felt something pulling at her wing. She looked up and saw her

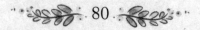

brother, Alfie, hovering above her, flapping his brown speckled wings like he'd been flying for ever.

"You're right, Katie. Blossom Wood is amazing," he twittered, his grin stretching from one long ear to the other. "I don't ever want to go home!"

Katie beamed back at her brother. He'd certainly changed his tune from when they'd first arrived! But she knew they'd have to go home soon, now that they'd helped the woodlanders. She wondered how she was going to break it to him.

"Sorry, Alfie, but we can't stay here," Alex said gently, overhearing their conversation and twirling over.

"But we can come back, don't worry," added Eva.

Alfie looked down and was quiet for

a moment, deep in thought. "As long as you promise this isn't just a dream?" he said eventually, his eyes wide.

Katie laughed and nodded. "Absolutely not — Blossom Wood is as real as real can be. And we'll be back — there's no doubt about that!"

Did You Know?

❀ Otters really do hold hands in the
water – it's very cute!

❀ Lily pads seem to float on water,
but really they are all part of one much
larger plant that has its roots
in the bottom of a lake or pond.

❀ When blown by the wind, dandelion
seeds can travel up to five miles before
reaching the ground!

❀ Goldfinches really do love to eat seeds.
If you have a garden or balcony, you
can hang up a bird feeder and fill it
with seeds – and watch many birds
come to visit!

Look out for more

The Owls of Blossom Wood

adventures!

❀ Would you like more animal
fun and facts?

❀ Fancy flying across the treetops in
the Owls of Blossom Wood game?

❀ Want sneak peeks of other
books in the series?

Then check out the Owls of
Blossom Wood website at:

theowlsofblossomwood.com